MARVEL

SPIDER-MAN

HOMECOMING

The Tangled Web of
SUPER
TECH

marvelkids.com

© 2017 MARVEL © 2017 CPII

Illustrations by Steve Kurth, Andy Smith, and Chris Sotomayor

Cover design by Carolyn Bull.

Little, Brown and Company
Hachette Book Group
1290 Avenue of the Americas, New York, NY 10104
Visit us at lb-kids.com
marvelkids.com

First Edition: June 2017

Little, Brown and Company is a division of Hachette Book Group, Inc. The Little, Brown name and logo are trademarks of Hachette Book Group, Inc.

The publisher is not responsible for websites (or their content) that are not owned by the publisher.

Library of Congress Control Number: 2017937398

ISBNs: 978-0-316-43822-3 (pbk.), 978-0-316-43823-0 (ebook), 978-0-316-43826-1 (ebook), 978-0-316-43824-7 (ebook)

Printed in the United States of America

CW

10 9 8 7 6 5 4 3 2

MARVEL
SPIDER-MAN
HOMECOMING

The Tangled Web of
SUPER
TECH

Adapted by R.R. Busse

Illustrations by Steve Kurth, Andy Smith, and Chris Sotomayor
Directed by Jon Watts
Produced by Kevin Feige and Amy Pascal
Based on the Screenplay by Jonathan Goldstein & John Francis Daley
and Jon Watts & Christopher Ford
and Chris McKenna & Erik Sommers

Ⓛ Ⓑ

Little, Brown and Company
New York Boston

Peter Parker is coming off the most intense experience of his life—helping Iron Man fight in the Avengers' Civil War as the high-flying Spider-Man.

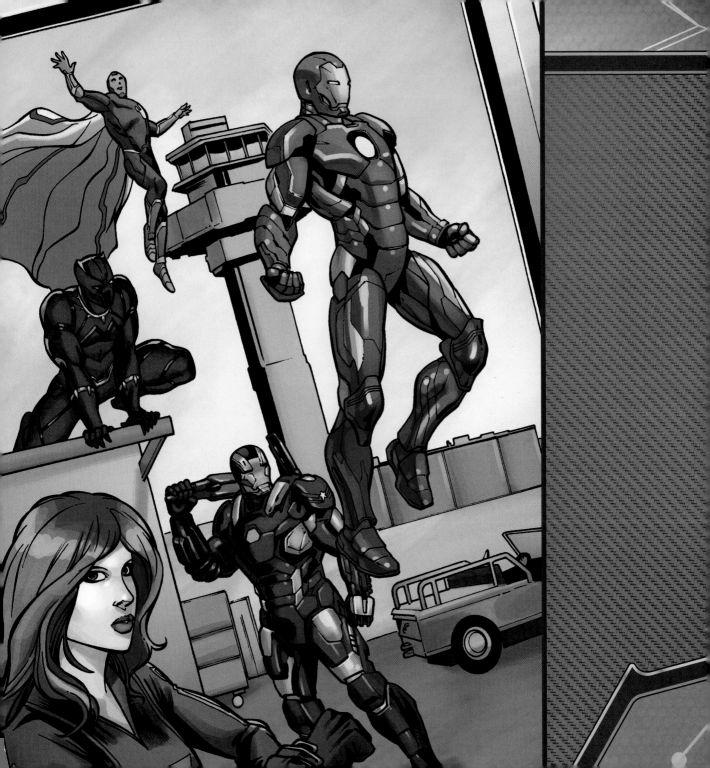

Now he's working on becoming a full-fledged Avenger, although he has a long way to go. Luckily for Peter, Tony Stark, aka Iron Man, is helping him out. So Peter gets rides in the Stark Industries limo and forms a little bit of a bond with Happy Hogan, Tony's driver, who is honestly never *that* happy.

Being friends with Tony means Peter has access to some awesome technology, including—one day, maybe—the state-of-the-art Avengers Tower, which soars over the New York City skyline.

Peter has come a long way from his original homemade suit. There's not a whole lot a high-school kid with a limited amount of money and sewing experience can piece together in secret, so it wasn't the most stylish costume in the world. Except for the hood...*that* was awesome.

But he had made custom goggles to perfectly suit his powers. They helped Peter focus when the action around him picked up speed.

His web shooters are his own design, and he makes his own superstrong webbing from scratch, usually under the table in his chemistry class.

The new suit comes straight from Tony Stark. It's high-tech, and he even kept the signature red and blue colors. *These* eyepieces react to Peter's face and outside factors, giving his mask some flexibility in a fight.

There are a lot of features to discover about *any* piece of Stark tech, and Peter's just the science whiz to do it.

What good is a spider without any webs? Spider-Man's webs are perfect for catching fleeing thieves, trapping muggers until the police arrive, or swinging through the city.

Peter's webs dissolve in about an hour. So even bad guys won't be stuck to sidewalks and lampposts forever.

Something Peter can do whenever he wants—in or out of his costume—is wall-crawling, one of Spider-Man's most useful abilities. He can use it to sneak up on bad guys, or even just creep them out. It's not every day you see a Super Hero hanging out on the ceiling.

He can also get to tall rooftops—perfect for surveillance and web-swinging. It's important that his costume doesn't get in the way of his natural wall-crawling, and his designs make sure he's able to scale sheer walls with no problem.

Other tools at Spider-Man's disposal are his tiny Spidey trackers. These little robotic spiders can cling to anyone, and avoid detection. All Spidey has to do is check on his holographic map, and he knows exactly where a mark is hiding.

Using all this amazing technology, Spider-Man can track down basically anyone, and swing in to save the day. Just ask the German chancellor.

With his friend Ned's help, Peter is even able to unlock upgrades to the suit Tony gave him to use. Tony had put more technology behind some safety measures, but Peter and Ned are good enough with tech to access the supersecret features.

For instance, the suit now includes high-tech imaging software! Spider-Man's suit has an advanced AI that helps him through different dangerous situations.

When there are people in danger, this software lets Peter know exactly where they are, how many people could be hurt, and how to best tackle the problem.

All the tech in the world doesn't mean Spider-Man can take on crime alone. Luckily, every once in a while, his mentor, Iron Man, is around to help him out of particularly tough jams.

But Tony Stark and Peter Parker aren't the only ones in the world who know how to use cutting-edge tech....

Adrian Toomes used to run a cleaning crew that cleaned up particularly huge messes—like the rubble from the end of the Battle of New York, when the Avengers assembled for the first time and pushed back the Chitauri invasion of Earth.

They found something extra special as they cleaned.

Working with a man known as the Tinkerer, Adrian was able to convert some technology from space into a dangerous new weapon that could take out Spider-Man for good.

The Tinkerer used to salvage with Toomes, but since they lost their valuable contracts to the government, he's been helping out on other projects. He's a technical genius.

He helped outfit Toomes's crew with powerful new gear. These gauntlets transform a normal guy like Herman into the Shocker—turning ordinary punches into superpowered assaults capable of knocking even Spider-Man out of a fight.

Of course, Toomes saved some of the best stuff for himself, robbing even more tech from delicate government shipments, and getting the better of Spider-Man more than once.

With razor-sharp talons and enormous mechanical wings, the Vulture is incredibly formidable because of his tech. He has enhanced vision thanks to his eerie, glowing green eyes.

Peter knows he's in for a fight, especially when the bad guys have equipment just as impressive as his. But at the end of the day, he has the determination to come out on top. After all, he's the amazing Spider-Man!